A Saint in Swindon

Fairlight Books

First published by Fairlight Books 2020

Fairlight Books
Summertown Pavilion, 18–24 Middle Way, Oxford, OX2 7LG

A CIP catalogue record for this book is available from the
British Library

1 2 3 4 5 6 7 8 9 10

ISBN 978-1-912054-20-6

www.fairlightbooks.com

Printed and bound by Clays Ltd.

Designed by Fairlight Books

Foreword

Members of reading groups often raise questions about how authors write, why they say what they say and who edits their work.

That's the way it has been for almost twenty years at the Swindon Artswords Reading Group, one of the town's many such groups. At monthly meetings, members question and challenge what authors have written.

But the authors are not there to answer their questions. Readers can only speculate.

So, at Swindon Artswords, a literature development project linked to Swindon Libraries and supported by the town's council and Arts Council England, we thought it might be a good idea to bring author and readers together, to 'close the circle', to enable readers to be commissioners of new literature as well as its eventual consumers.

It was hoped that we could create an opportunity for readers to address all their questions directly to an author and, most significantly, to get an insight into where ideas come from; what the author wants and listens to; what the editing process is like; who decides what stays and what goes; and who creates the look of the book.

To this end we asked readers in Swindon if they would like to commission an author to write a story. They said yes! So we asked a prizewinning author if she would like to write a short story, based broadly on some of the preferences and ideas of Swindon reading groups.

Alice Jolly was the author of choice. We were delighted that she accepted our invitation, even with its attendant risks.

And so it was that in June 2019 Alice came to Swindon and met members of Artswords and Swindon Libraries reading groups, and the process began.

Notebook and pen in hand, Alice sat silently in the meeting room, a former calf shed at Lower Shaw Farm on the outskirts of Swindon, and let the readers talk. Enthusiastically, they told her about the kind of books they liked and what they hoped to see in a story, and even offered ideas of their own. Dutifully, Alice made notes, thanked the readers and went on her way.

Three months later she sent us a draft, explaining that the short story had become a longer one.

Well, the undersigned for one was not about to complain, especially since he found the newly written story unputdownable. Members of the reading group, like the keen commissioners they were, received the story with glee... but also a question or three.

So author Alice was invited back to the farm meeting room for a readers' response session, which turned into a delightful but disciplined editing exercise. Characters were discussed, themes were identified and explored, and streets and areas of the town were even given their rightful names.

Alice declared herself 'genuinely impressed by the level of debate and the ideas offered'. And, for their part, the commissioners in the readers' group were very happy too with what the author had produced.

So happy, in fact, that they quickly decided the story should be shared with a wider audience and a proper agent and publisher must be found.

The search was on: possible publishers were approached and slush piles were circumnavigated, because we wanted the book out in time for a big celebratory launch at the Swindon Spring Festival of Literature and the Arts in May 2020.

After one or two false starts, we were lucky to find a vibrant young publishing company whose one aim – 'to celebrate quality writing and promote the best of new and contemporary literary fiction' – suggested that they were precisely the kind of outfit we needed.

That publisher was Fairlight Books. Their informed, efficient and friendly team, especially Louise Boland, Urška Vidoni, Laura Shanahan and Bradley Thomas, have been a delight to work with and we thank them for meeting the tight publishing schedule with such good cheer.

With efficiency to match and equal good cheer, Alice's agent Victoria Hobbs and her colleague Jessica Sinyor at A M Heath Ltd also happily embraced the idea of getting *A Saint in Swindon* published.

Maybe, like us, none of them could wait to share this story, and its backstory, with other readers.

We hope you will enjoy it and will share news of *A Saint in Swindon* with others, too, so that it becomes a deserved bestseller, with some of its hoped-for profits going towards further literature development work in Swindon.

Thank you for reading this far and happy onward reading!

Matt Holland – Literature Development Worker for Swindon Artswords, which is grateful for support for its work from Arts Council England, Swindon Borough Council, Swindon Libraries, Lower Shaw Farm and the Swindon Spring Festival of Literature and the Arts.

A Saint in Swindon

It was evening when the stranger arrived in the town. Everyone assumed that he had travelled here by train and then walked along Whitehouse Road heading towards Ferndale, but the truth is that no one knows. At the time, those days and weeks seemed plump and loud, full of their own importance. Each minute separate and swollen, the hours shouting significant messages, stating their meaning clearly.

But now that I look through the notes I made at that time, now that I try to write it all down, everything is strangely foggy. That lost world appears as though seen at some great distance, the images distorted and discoloured. It's like tuning one of those old radios. The reception is crackly and won't come clear no matter how many times I turn the dial. Whatever I might say would definitely be shouted down, if anyone now could find the energy for shouting.

What can I say for certain? The date, perhaps. Five years ago, the summer of 2030. Not an age of innocence. No. More like an overheated world of childhood inhabited by toddling and tetchy adults. All of us like overripe fruit, still shiny on the outside yet rotten within. I can't explain. It was the best of times, it was the worst of times. That's what I might have said, but I hadn't read Dickens then.

*

He came to our town, that much is certain, and we – Phil and I – were expecting him. He'd telephoned earlier to ask if we had any rooms. As our B&B, Hunter's Grove, caters primarily for business customers, and it was early July, we did have a room free, so we agreed the booking verbally. Since it was short notice, Phil didn't take a deposit from him.

We were glad enough to have guests. The B&B business is fiercely competitive. I had hoped that boutique hotels would be just a fad, but there's no way back now. I personally would have been happy to cut the clutter and say goodbye to some of the patterned carpet.

I'd have been more than happy to experiment with upholstered headboards, metallic paint and faux-fur rugs – I can layer cushions as well as the next woman – but Phil doesn't want any of that. 'All just a marketing trick.' That's his opinion.

Our B&B is squat and stern 1930s red brick, which may not be exciting, but it's only a mile from the station and it has three off-road parking spaces. It also has a Garden Room and a terrace for the exclusive use of guests. The door handles are polished and we always have fresh flowers from the garden. 'All of which is worth a lot more than heart-shaped chocolates,' Phil says.

I digress. All the best writers do. It was mid-afternoon when our guest came to the front door. I'd just done the hoovering and I was in the hall, on the phone, trying to sort out the internet. I remember his shadow appeared through the frosted glass and the bell rang with a particularly insistent, clamouring note. Well, no, perhaps not. I must keep things clear. It was a normal day and he appeared to be an ordinary guest. I clicked off the phone and pushed the Hoover into the cupboard in the back passage.

At the time, I remember assuming he was in his late thirties or early forties. Later I decided he was older. He carried a blue holdall. The bag looked heavy and bulged oddly, but he lifted it with ease. I asked him to fill out the usual form, but he wrote only his name in large and careless writing – Jack MacKafka. I remember his forearms as he stretched out his hand to take the key – tight and tanned, the hands precise and well-scrubbed. His fingers fumbled against mine as I passed him the key. I may have giggled in a childish way. I wanted to make a joke but couldn't think of one.

He had dark hair and was clean-shaven. His mouth was firm with a slight upward curve at the sides, a permanent smile. I imagined clear, questioning eyes, but it was hard to get an accurate sense of him as he was wearing dark glasses and a denim baseball cap. Overall, he was nothing out of the ordinary. Perhaps there was a slight whiff of adventure about him. You could imagine him clambering up a mountain, white-water rafting, hang-gliding, something like that.

The conversation was brief. He said he'd be staying four days and he'd pay in advance, in cash. People don't usually do that, but I didn't give it much thought. The flat roof of the garden room was beginning to leak. Phil and I were putting money aside. The months of July and August can be quiet no matter what discount you offer.

He asked if our B&B did food other than breakfast. On the website it does say 'other meals available by arrangement' – I don't like to be tied down to too much cooking, but I'll always do it if the time is available. I charge £6 for a ploughman's lunch and £10 for a main course and pudding in the evening. I make everything fresh. Usually I'm cooking for Phil anyway, so it isn't much extra work. It was arranged that our guest would have supper. I said that it would be served in the dining room. He asked if I could send up a tray, and I agreed to that.

*

I put him in the back bedroom because that is our largest and quietest room. It's reached by a separate staircase opposite the sitting room door. That evening Phil carried the tray up, knocked on the door and left it outside the room. Later I went into the garden to hang out some washing. The familiar view from the lawn – rooves, trees, fences, vacant windows, looping telegraph wires – was lit by a blue and drowsy evening light. A lawn mower moaned from a distant garden. I looked up at our guest's room above the troublesome flat roof of the garden room. I noticed the curtains were closed, but our guest *had* looked tired, a little ragged. Maybe he'd decided to turn in early. It was that kind of weather, that time of year.

Next morning, he didn't come down to breakfast. Guests are told clearly that breakfast is from 7 to 9.30. I like to get everything cleared and sorted by 10 so I can start on the beds and the laundry. I went up at 9.35. When I knocked on the door, he opened it immediately. He looked exactly the same as the day before, except that he had exchanged the blue polo shirt for a similar shirt in grey. He was still wearing the dark glasses and the baseball cap. He said he was sorry not to have come down.

'Would it be possible to send something up on a tray?' he asked.

Breakfast in bed is not a service we offer but I felt he might be unwell so I decided to do as he requested.

Then I said, 'Any plans for the day?'

'Yes,' he said. 'My plan is to stay in bed and read.'

'Oh,' I said. 'Oh. Sounds lovely.'

Obviously he was unwell or exhausted. I

returned with the tray, and mentioned that I could also bring up a ploughman's lunch for him later. He agreed to that and asked if the same would be possible for supper. That was all the conversation we had. But I did notice a pile of books on the desk near the door. *Tess of the d'Urbervilles*, *Crime and Punishment*, *Heart of Darkness*. Odd choices. I'd have thought he'd be reading mainly detectives.

*

The next morning, he didn't come down to breakfast again. I was worried then about his health. Phil told me I was being soft. He shook his bald head, waved a plump finger at me in the usual way. He thinks that's funny but it's just irritating. 'You start serving breakfast in bed and you'll be doing it for everyone.' I understood his point, but he doesn't acknowledge the power of TripAdvisor. One bad review and you can lose your business. [1]

Anyway, I thought that our reading guest was unwell and he certainly wasn't doing any harm. Maybe all that rock climbing and white-water rafting had tired him out. So I took the tray up at breakfast, and then again at lunch, and then again at supper. Each time the food was all eaten up. I never saw him at any of those times. But in the evening there was enough cash on the tray to pay for the meals, plus a couple of pounds extra.

The next morning I was clearing up the dining room after Mr Cashman, one of our regular guests, had left, when my friend Susan appeared at the door. She lives in one of the houses behind ours and an alleyway runs through from her street to Hunter's Grove. A gate leads from that alleyway into our garden and I always leave it unlocked. Susan often pops round in the morning when she knows I'll be clearing up after breakfast. Sometimes Carmen or Jamila turns up as well. The four of us have a book group, but it's mostly wine and chat.

Susan wanted to discuss what the book group should read next. I'd go for a psychological thriller, but Susan wouldn't want that. Since her marriage broke up, she's gone mad for Open University literature courses. She likes to beat us over the head with the virtues of study. Read your book, tidy your bedroom, eat your greens. I don't mind because I take a look at the book she suggests and, unless it looks like something I'd actually enjoy, I reserve it at the library. At least that way I'm not paying. You can generally find a summary online if you need one.

'Carmen wants to try a dystopian novel. You know what she's like,' Susan said. She began to tell me what dystopian meant but I put a lid on that. Does she think I'm stupid? Anyway, it was because of that conversation that I mentioned our guest.

'Reading?' Susan said. 'All day? Just reading?'

'Well, yes. Why not?'

'Just seems a bit odd. So what's he reading?'

I told her what I'd seen.

'Ah,' Susan said. 'Studying the nineteenth century, maybe? Considering the opposition between human choice and the role of fate in the unfolding of human life.'

That's how she is. Guardian of the Books. She's matey with the town librarians. At our last book group, Susan told us more than we wanted to know about the Dewey Decimal System. I don't mind – or not much. She found it hard to move on after the divorce. Her husband had been improving his French. She was called Geraldine – although she may have been Irish rather than French, now I think about it. It's hard for Susan, although she doesn't do much to help herself with those orthopaedic shoes and her hair hanging limp.

'I'll take that tray up,' she said. 'Maybe I can see what else he's reading.'

'No. No need. I can deal with that, thanks.'

*

That summer it was hot enough to strip paint. My feet were swelling like potatoes. At night, Phil was tossing, turning, snorting, unable to get any sleep. A hosepipe ban had been announced, but Phil went out after dark to water the garden. He wasn't letting the roses go. The next morning Susan came round again and Carmen was with her. Carmen is Spanish, or maybe Portuguese. Passionate, she says. Hysterical might be more accurate. I was busy putting the laundry on and Phil was washing up.

'I don't know,' I told her. 'How could I know what he's doing?'

Carmen does what Susan and I refer to as 'pick-and-mix religion'. The Catholics, the Church of England, the Muslims and the Buddhists. She's been through the lot. In the modern age there may be religious tolerance, but if you mix crystal reading or tarot up with Christ or Allah or whoever else, then you can cause offence. We've tried to tell her but she never gets the point. Now she's become confused between our guest and her latest religious theories.

'But it is obvious,' she said. 'Ve-ry clear. I se-e-e it, of course. This is happening often now. Many people are turning to God. It's due to the vanity and the shallow values of our modern world.'

'Carmen, he's reading books,' Susan said.

Carmen has long dark hair and eyes that could nail you, dangling, from a wall. She wears swinging gold earrings and they shook now as she nodded her head. 'Yes, studying. That is an essential part of the contemplative life. He needs to shut himself away from a-a-ll the world. In a society obsessed by money, sex and power, it's only through prayer that you can find freedom. He may well be a monk or a priest.'

'He was wearing a baseball cap.'

'The spiritual life takes many different forms.'

Susan rolled her eyes as she carried plates over to the sink. In the book group we were often left uncertain as to whether Carmen had an overly active imagination or whether she was just plain stupid. *Liza of Lambeth* is about the importance of proper household hygiene. *The Secret History* is about managing your money carefully. Jamila tried to keep things pleasant by insisting that it's just about what you see in a book. You need to read between the lines. That's the joy of novels.

When Carmen starts, I usually pour more wine and try to bring things round to local gossip. Did you hear about the man who drove for ten miles down the M4 in the wrong direction? Foxes in the bins again on Ferndale Road. A woman in Stratton St Margaret has got a pet alligator in her garden pond. No, really. Susan tends to be more confrontational, but she never gets anywhere. Carmen is always sure of her views. We are all too literal, too narrow, too blind to see beyond the surface. Often Carmen half closes her eyes and says something annoying like 'How can you build the future if you do not dream?'

I don't know what future she is considering. I mean, we're fifty-something women, living in a suburb of a regular sort of town. What are the possibilities? I'm not saying that the only option is to slide down towards the grave. It doesn't have to be hearing aids, corn plasters and trousers with elasticated waists. I certainly don't see myself in that way. I run a successful small business. I may have lost my waist but I take good care of myself. But the future? I mean, really?

*

The trays kept going up and down. Phil shook his head at me but said nothing. One morning I banged on the door and said, 'Feeling better now?' Our guest popped his head out and said that he was fine, that he'd never felt ill. The next morning I saw him briefly as he was putting some money on the tray. 'You're certainly hard at work,' I said. 'Studying for an exam, are you? English Literature, is it? How much longer do you have?' He did not look at me as he retreated, but he did say quite clearly that he wasn't studying for an exam. Susan said he was probably a teacher preparing a new course. I tried that the next morning. 'So where is it that you teach, then?' Reversing, he denied that he was a teacher. So what was he doing?

Jamila came round on Friday. She only ever comes on Fridays as she is busy at the hospital on other days. She's a medical assistant but she's hoping to train as a nurse. She'd obviously been talking to Susan because she'd been to the library to get those same books – *Tess of the d'Urbervilles*, *Crime and Punishment* and *Heart of Darkness*. She also had a copy of *Cider with Rosie* as she thought we should give that a try. She won't let the Guardian of the Books win every battle.

'Reading Conrad,' she said, shaking her head. '*Heart of Darkness*. A disturbing book. Also *Crime and Punishment*. Do you think he's ill? You really have a duty to insist on a doctor.'

'I don't think he's ill,' I said.

'There are many different kinds of illness.'

'Yes – but what kind of illness gives you a hearty appetite?'

'No. You can't make that kind of assumption. You really can't.'

Jamila is that type of person. Kind – but interfering kind. That's nurses for you. Small, tidy, bustling. Cute little pearl earrings and her hair in the neatest of bobs. Even her shorts are carefully ironed. She loves to be part of a minor crisis, to be needed, to step in and sort things out in a caring, brisk, no-nonsense way. I'm being nasty, I know, but it can get wearing. Since I didn't want to talk to her any more, I picked up *Tess of the d'Urbervilles* and read the back. I also took a look at *Cider with Rosie*.

'I might give these two a go.'

Jamila didn't want me to take those books, but she couldn't say no.

'I really think you should go into the room, check on him,' she said.

'It isn't my business to disturb the guests.'

'So he had books in the bag?'

'Well, he must have done. Where else would he get them?'

'It was a big bag?'

'No, medium-sized. But lumpy.'

'Lumpy how?'

*

Lumpy? It wasn't any of our business. Phil reminded me of that. Stained sheets, sobbing in the night, bouts of vomiting, people leaving at 3am. All that is part of the job. Once someone ate the potpourri in our hall. Sometimes people stuff their socks in the tissue box. When I went in for decorative pebbles in bowls – my one nod to boutique – someone put them in the toilet and another person added some flowers to make a miniature garden.

You don't ask questions. Reading Conrad or Dostoyevsky is not a sign of mental illness.

People come and go. It's never a good idea to get involved. But it was strange how our guest never came out of his room. The trays went up the next day and the day after. It was the punishing heat. It made people turn funny.

I sat in the sitting room reading *Tess*. Now that was a story to transport you to another place – although actually it's all in our part of the world. Susan and Jamila kept turning up, offering to take up the trays since I was busy reading, but I wasn't having any of that.

It wasn't my business to ask questions about our guest but, as the days passed, I was trying to work it out. Phil would usually have told me to put a stop to the whole thing, to tell our reader that I wouldn't take up any more trays. But three other bookings had been cancelled. No one wanted to travel in that sticky and restless heat.

Phil didn't exactly criticise Susan, Jamila and Carmen. That isn't his way – but I knew what he thought. Women and their daft ideas. We should never have given them the vote. But soon Phil had theories himself. It started when he was reading the local paper. He told me about his concerns while he was helping with the washing-up. The police were looking for a man in connection with a violent robbery at a service station on the M4.

'Why didn't he let you see his face?' he said.

'It was hot. People wear caps.'

'Wearing a cap and sunglasses inside?'

'Oh Phil, do be careful. You've broken that jug.'

*

Don't get involved, that's what Phil said, but we were involved and I had my suspicions. I'd got to the end of *Tess* by then. That book finishes up in a guest house in the West Country. Surely that was not a coincidence. Was our reader sending us a message? Why does anyone hide in a B&B? He couldn't just be reading. No one just lies in bed and reads. Not day after day.

Maybe he was a celebrity? Or someone who had won the lottery? Maybe it was the press he was hiding from, not the police. I didn't say that to Phil, who was still certain that crime explained everything – but then they issued a photofit of the service station robber and he had jowls. I'd not seen much of our reader but he definitely didn't have jowls. So that was the end of that – or so I hoped.

Then a body was found in London. Some poor woman battered, her body dismembered and hidden in a cellar. It seemed the murder had happened just over a week ago. The suspect was slim and in his late thirties. Phil wondered whether he should go to the police. I thought it was all to do with lack of sleep. You can't assume it's only men who commit crimes. Women do often murder men – and sometimes with good reason. Though personally I'd have taken Alec d'Urberville over Angel Clare any time.

*

For ten whole days it went on and I kept myself busy with the trays. I'd read *Cider with Rosie* by then and I was on to *Heart of Darkness*. Certainly it was hot as the Congo in Hunter's Grove. No one wanted to do anything except sit with the curtains drawn. Plus the internet was still off. Phil had rung about it several times. Apparently the problem was all down the street. I wondered why Jamila thought the Conrad book was to do with mental breakdown. Reading between the lines, it seemed to me a romantic book. I had to drink a lot of lemonade to cool myself down.

But then Tuesday came around again – I'm always busy on a Tuesday afternoon. I'm not sure I want to write down this bit of the story. It doesn't show me in a particularly favourable light and it isn't relevant to our reading guest. But since I am being honest perhaps I should say. Anyway, none of it matters now. We're all past caring. So every Tuesday afternoon I go round to see Len. He's a builder who lives on our street and he's got a lovely detached house with a garden room. His roof is not flat and turning rotten like ours. I did warn Phil against that roof but, unfortunately, he's a master of the false economy.

Anyway, Len's wife died five years ago, so I go to see him for the afternoon on Tuesdays. Afterwards he runs a bath for me, just the right temperature, with lavender bubbles. Then he makes a cup of tea with some chocolate-chunk biscuits. What I'm trying to say is that I have sex with Len on Tuesdays. It's not a secret. Phil knows – half the street knows. Len likes sex. Phil lost interest a while back. Tea with Len, cider with Rosie. What's the difference?

So anyway, I was out on Tuesday afternoon but I came back slightly earlier than I might usually have done as Len had to go to an emergency dental appointment. One of his teeth broke – not on a chocolate-chunk biscuit but on a piece of toffee. He's always had a sweet tooth. I didn't mind. I was reading *Crime and Punishment* by then and I wanted to get back to it.

I came down the alleyway and up to the kitchen door, and there were Jamila and Carmen. They certainly weren't bothering to hide their crime, or contemplating the problem of guilt. I knew immediately what they were about. They were intending to go up and knock on the door, ask our reader some questions, break into his privacy. I told them to clear out – in a pleasant manner. Carmen with her wretched crystal reading and Jamila with her endless watery-eyed concern.

As Carmen left she was rattling on about religion again. 'A sign of the evil times in which we live. Money changers in the temple. The reader in the bedroom. You can see the link, can't you?'

I couldn't, but I made a mental note that if I needed to go out again I'd ask Susan to keep an eye on things. At least she could be trusted not to interfere. If I'm honest, I took the whole thing badly because our reader was mine – he belonged to me and I didn't want anyone else getting their hands on him. If anyone was going into that room, it would be me.

*

Then that same evening I saw him. He was waiting for me as I brought the supper tray up. He seemed exceptionally tall standing at the door. He looked like the kind of man who is photographed by the *Daily Mail*. He was sliding out of the door frame, or photo, slightly furtive and entirely captivating. Again, he was wearing the cap and sunglasses. I nearly stumbled with the tray. He had jeans on and another shirt. How many shirts did he have? He'd been in there ten days.

'Thank you,' he said. 'It's very comfortable here. I feel like I could stay forever.'

I glowed at that. I do take pride in Hunter's Grove. He had chosen us over themed bedrooms, unique selling points and statement wallpaper. He was not a man to be seduced by locally sourced sausages, pressed linen sheets and fluffy robes.

'But I was just wondering,' he said.

'Of course,' I said. 'What do you need?'

I could feel my heart beginning to rush. I'd never been close to a celebrity before.

'I was just wondering – do you have a library card?'

'A library card?'

For a moment I was stumped, but then I realised that he wouldn't want to go to a bookshop. That was too public. Celebrities probably do use libraries because it is easy to hide behind all those shelves. They're only normal people after all.

'Yes,' I said. 'Yes, I do. Did you want some books?'

'Oh yes,' he said.

'Actually, we have an exceptionally good library,' I told him. That was the truth. For forty years this town was campaigning to get the library moved out of the portacabins. Now we've got a prizewinning modern building with long windows, a spiral staircase, blonde wood, comfortable chairs. It is a palace of books and the team there do a fantastic job. It must be one of the best in the country.

'I could write down some titles for you, leave them on the tray?' he said.

'Fine,' I said. 'Yes. Fine.'

I moved a little closer. I wanted to look inside the room. I wanted to be close to him.

'What about the room? It must need a clean.'

'No. It's no problem. Although maybe some clean sheets?'

'Yes. I can do that immediately if you want.'

Now I'll get into that room, I thought. I'll see what's in there.

'No,' he said. 'No need. Just leave the sheets at the door.'

'Fine. Fine.'

'Laundry?'

I didn't want him having to put up with dirty clothes.

'That would be kind. Thank you very much.'

The way he said that was so personal, so particular.

'Yes, of course,' I said. 'Of course. Just leave anything you want outside the door.'

'Thank you,' he said. 'Thank you. Sorry – your name is?'

'Janey.' My name sounded exceptional then. He was mine, all mine.

*

The next day people I barely knew started turning up, asking questions. That was Carmen's fault. They don't call her Radio Ferndale for nothing.

Those people all wanted to know about our reader. Could they pop upstairs and have a chat with him? Perhaps he might be able to recommend a good book? At first, I tried to be polite. I even made cups of coffee and slices of toast. But then people in dusty boots walked straight through the reception and three women, mad as cackling witches, had a vocal argument outside the back door at 9pm.

It was all getting too much. An elderly man turned up and stood under the window, scraping away on a violin like a cat with stomach cramps. After that I began to take a firmer line. When twenty more arrived, I told them to go away and mind their own business. I found it embarrassing really, but Susan was with me and she backed me up. I was grateful to her and I suppose that is why, after they'd all gone, I showed her the list. *The Brothers Karamazov*, *Vanity Fair*, *Madame Bovary*.

'Obviously a scholar,' she said. 'He's probably writing an academic paper.'

'No. I asked him about that,' I said, but Susan took no notice.

'Maybe something to do with the role of the individual within the confines of society. Or perhaps the changing role of women. No need for you to go to the library. I'll go. Some of those books might have to be reserved. I don't think there are many readers round here wanting those kinds of books.'

That annoyed me. We all agree that people shouldn't be negative about our town. Susan is always furious when she hears negative comments but she'll happily say those same things herself. Anyway, I wasn't having *her* go to the library – he hadn't asked *her* – but she wouldn't be put off. Finally, we agreed to go together.

*

As soon as we came back from the library, Carmen turned up. She was waving her hands and her earrings. Her mad eyes were rolling and she was rambling on about the inner light and the path to salvation.

'You need to stop telling people,' I told her.

'Me? I didn't tell anyone. People just know. They kno-o-w. They can feel that he's somebody special. He is praying for our souls, he will be our salvation.'

That's how she went on. Can you believe it? Then she picked up a sock.

'Is this his washing?' she said.

'What if it is? People have got a right to some privacy, haven't they?' I tried to snatch the pile of washing, but she'd already got hold of one of his socks and was handling it in an extremely strange manner, as though it was a small, frightened animal. She wasn't exactly stroking it but she might have been.

'You can tell,' she said. 'You can tell. The smell is so fresh. A heavenly smell.'

'No, Carmen.' I said. 'That's the pine fabric conditioner I use.'

She started to go through the books we had got. I didn't want Carmen touching them. We'd got them for him. We'd also got *Far from the Madding Crowd*. The last Hardy was so good that I wanted to read all of them now. Carmen picked up *The Brothers Karamazov* and looked at the back. 'Themes of God, free will and morality. There's even a monk. Definitely the book for me.' She held it against her.

'Right, I'll have these.' I took *Vanity Fair* and the Hardy.

Susan wasn't happy about any of this. She was the Guardian of the Books.

'Well, he can't read all of those at once,' Carmen said.

*

Later that day I went into town and bought a couple of magazines, plus the *Mail* for Phil. The *Mail* was full of the heatwave. What a sizzler. Britain in meltdown. Pictures of bikini-clad women jumping through sprinklers, news of wildfires and a shortage of lettuces. Apparently it was all caused by a plume of hot air from the Sahara. Phil wasn't interested in that. He wanted to know about the murderer in London. There was a photofit of him now. 'Doesn't that look like our guest?'

I wanted to say no because I was fed up with Phil interfering, but I wondered if, actually, our reader did look like the photofit.

'I should go to the police,' Phil said.

'You're not doing that,' I said. 'Staying in bed and reading isn't a crime.'

Phil doesn't like to be told, but he knew I was right. Still, he wasn't going to give up. Women can't be relied upon – we are overly emotional, gullible, hysterical. He'd also probably guessed that I'd taken a fancy to our reader, so now he wanted to play the big man. He'd have done better to get the internet fixed.

Instead he went round to the library. He never normally reads any novels. 'Why is it better to read books than watch football?' That's what he says. He used to be in engineering before he retired and started meddling. Retirement – twice as much husband and half as much money. In sickness and in health, but never lunch. Anyway, science and facts, that's what he does – but since we'd become library addicts, he didn't want to miss out. He hoped to find technical books about crime but they didn't have them, so he had to get true crime instead. Truman Capote, Kate Summerscale and Gordon Burn.

'Full of good ideas for how to find out about criminals,' he said.

I took another look at the photofit in the newspaper but I couldn't be sure, so I turned to the magazines instead. As soon as I began to look through those photographs of celebrities, I knew. That was exactly the look our reader had. Celebrities were often photographed on beaches or at airports wearing chinos and polo shirts and dark glasses.

He was one of those people, I knew it. And I knew how pressured those lives could be. You can't even step outside your own front door without being photographed. If he'd gone to a famous hotel, the press would have known he was there. Hunter's Grove was the obvious bolthole for a person like that. Quiet, discreet but extremely comfortable. Celebrities don't often come to our town, but he had chosen us. I was not going to betray his confidence.

It was too hot to betray anyone. I sat in the lounge with the blinds down. From there I could see the back staircase and ensure that he wasn't disturbed. People still kept turning up. Mainly it was just all the nosy people in our town, but a group of sociology students also gathered at the door wanting to study the effect of reading and solitude on human health. What is he doing? Is this a protest of some sort? Can you describe his state of mind to us?

'Look, he's probably just trying to read his way through one of those Top 100 Novels lists,' I said. 'Please, I'm busy. This really isn't any of your business.'

But that group hadn't turned out of our gate when a man with a colander on his head showed up holding a banner about protecting whales. Lost, deranged, or both? He was trying to press a box of frozen fish fingers into my hands. I told him to get lost. Then I put notices on the front and back doors telling people not to ring the bell, but they still did. *Far from the Madding Crowd*? I wouldn't have minded myself.

*

Our reader wanted more books. A list was placed on the tray. *The Bell Jar* by Sylvia Plath, *The Castle* by Franz Kafka, and *Animal Farm* and *1984* by George Orwell. Initially Susan was uncertain about this list. Her theory about the nineteenth century had been proven wrong but, after a few moments of doubt, she soon started to support our reader again. Novels are not always about pleasure. We need to be prepared to explore the darker side of life. She thought, in fact, she might perhaps write her Master's degree thesis on Kafka and other existential novels.

I didn't tell her my thoughts on *Vanity Fair*. I'd enjoyed that book so much I didn't want to share it with her. Becky Sharp – now she was an operator. I could learn a few lessons from her. I'd started to keep notes about what I was reading. When I was finally able to talk to our reader, I didn't want to forget any of the details.

'You don't make notes for book group,' Susan said in a lemon-juice tone.

'No. But I've discovered I like writing. I might write a novel myself sometime.'

She gave me a look full of such contempt that I felt a little shrivelled.

'Perhaps just a short story.'

People kept coming round. I didn't have the energy to tell them to go away and I didn't want to be unpleasant. I just left the kitchen door open so they could come and go as they wanted. I couldn't blame people for gathering there because I have a large fan in the kitchen and the room is up against the garden fence, next to a large tree, so it tends to stay cooler than other places. They often discussed Orwell. Was it the case that his dystopian nightmare had arrived, but that it had been caused by mobile phones and one-day delivery rather than a totalitarian government? They asked Phil for his view on the struggle between the individual and the system in *1984*. 'Best to stick to 2030.' That was his response. From my chair in the sitting room, I kept a close eye on the back stairs.

Sometimes I could also hear Susan, Jamila and Carmen arguing. Nursey-nursey Jamila was still determined that our reader was ill. Reading Kafka was definitely evidence of a disturbed mind. It was our duty to get him to a doctor. But Carmen had the Kafka as well and she didn't agree. Not if you read between the lines. Could Jamila not see? Is it not the case that all mental illness is actually spiritual hunger? Clearly the book was about the meaningless nature of modern society and our need to withdraw from the world to rediscover the religious life, to find truth and freedom.

'And *Animal Farm*,' Carmen said. 'Ve-e-ry interesting on the subject of animal welfare.'

I held *The Castle* up against my face and tried to ignore them. Susan came in occasionally to talk to me. She herself was enjoying trying some new books, but still she felt that our reader should have stuck to the nineteenth century. Realism and the exploration of moral values were really the proper business of the novel. Reading between the lines was all very well, but not without proper guidance. I wasn't listening as I was into the last pages of *The Castle*. I don't think that most people would consider romance to be key to that book, but I enjoyed it as a story written with great tenderness.

*

Another list of books came down on a tray. Susan and Jamila went to the library to get them without telling Carmen. I didn't go because the heat was affecting my mind and I was too busy with *The Bell Jar*. As soon as they came back I looked through the books. *Lady Chatterley's Lover*, *The Crack-Up*, *Portrait of a Lady*, *Jane Eyre*. He was trying to send me a message. That was obvious. Susan was sniffy about *Lady Chatterley's Lover*. Everyone knew that book was one of Lawrence's weaker efforts, and anyway no one read Lawrence now.

Phil tried to shut them up. He'd already exhausted true crime in the library. *Crime and Punishment* had looked so promising but by the end he was sorely disappointed. It wasn't like a proper detective. I was in the kitchen with Susan doing one of the trays when he said that. We both shook our heads and sighed. Some people are just so ignorant.

After that Phil moved on to police procedurals. It turned out that they had as much interesting information as the true crime books. He was relying on them to get the answers. He sat in the chair opposite me and talked about toxicology and ballistics, but I wasn't listening. Instead I dreamed of other lives. Our reader was probably late forties and I was mid-fifties. Many men like a mature woman. I was reading *Madame Bovary* and understanding how our small domestic life had stifled me. I was always a woman with a wider dream.

Phil was angry with me. 'Why aren't the sheets washed? What are you doing about the internet? You can't just defrost ready meals for our guest. You've never done that before. You always did everything fresh.' Standards were slipping and I didn't care. If our reader could spend all day in bed, then surely I could sit in a chair and read? That's not a crime. I just wanted some peace and quiet. A bell jar? I'd happily have put one over my head.

*

Things might have been different if we'd had more to do. But it was that summer when they banned the use of cars and grounded all flights. We'd known it would come, but we'd always thought there'd be one more year. They had to act because old people were dying from the heat and the crops were all burnt up. Still, we knew it was just while the heat lasted. After that it would all go back to how it was before. Scaremongering, fake news. Even the station was closed because the railway lines had buckled and broken. The days can be long when you can't go anywhere.

I was also worried about Phil. Before the post stopped, he'd ordered himself a home fingerprinting kit and he was reading up on how the decomposition of bodies is affected by heat. He'd even been to the police station, but they were not particularly interested because by then the water had gone down and the police were supervising people in their efforts to bring water up in buckets from the River Ray, and even from the canal, which took a long time when no cars were allowed.

Still the trays went up, the cash was pushed under the side of an empty plate, the laundry was done. The lists of books came down. *Pride and Prejudice*, *Howards End*, *The Great Gatsby*, *Dr Zhivago*. We had to keep them hidden now. People would come in from the garden and ask questions. More than twenty tents had been pitched out there, all crammed up tightly together, far too close to Phil's roses. I'd told them that our garden is not a campsite, but they didn't listen. They all wanted to know what books our reader had asked for because they wanted to read those same books. Since there were not enough copies to go around they ended up reading the Bible instead. It turns out you can always find a copy of the Bible somewhere. Also, Carmen was out there all the time, talking about the spiritual life and how we must give up the temptations of the physical world. Groups gathered to discuss the contemplative life and to express their thanks to our reader for taking on the great burden of our sins. Many people wanted to join him in prayerful silence and seclusion. Talk about *The Crack-Up*. Why did no one ever tell me that madness can be infectious?

Susan was increasingly worried. All this was happening because so many people were reading books which they could easily misunderstand. Readers really needed the structure of an Open University course or a book group. Otherwise they could get the wrong idea, lose their moral compass. Perhaps Oscar Wilde was right when he said that the good should end well and the bad badly? In challenging times, surely that should be the meaning of fiction?

I nodded and smiled, but I wasn't listening. I was reading *Jane Eyre* by then. I'd read it at school and hadn't enjoyed it at all. What a Girl Guide she was. Now I saw it quite differently. The story took over my whole mind, but still I put the book aside to take up the trays. Sometimes I stood outside the door, listening, willing him to open it and let me in. I never heard a sound.

*

At night the temperature never dropped. I lay in bed and dreamed of him. He was blind and his hand had been injured in a fire, so I was nursing him. I was a mad woman in an attic, raging and screaming, longing to be let out. The two of us were running naked through woodland near Nottingham in defiance of the horrors of mechanisation. We were covering ourselves in garlands of wild flowers. It was the heat. We burned, burned, burned like fabulous roman candles. It was more than anyone could bear.

I started on *The Portrait of a Lady*. Phil had given up telling me to get the housework done. There were no other guests now anyway. One day Len came round and sat uncertainly in the armchair opposite me. He wanted to remind me that it was Tuesday – perhaps I had forgotten? Tuesday. You know. I found him tiresome. Despite the stoppages, he was busy. The dry ground was causing cracks to open up in walls, so he was replastering and even putting in props. So many people wanted bookshelves now. It was hard to find enough planks. I think that's what he said.

Phil offered Len a cup of tea. 'Tuesday,' he said. 'Tuesday.' He's always been fond of Len. I told them both that I was busy reading. I couldn't leave Isabel Archer in the lurch. What exactly was so wrong with the man she married? I told Len I might have time to speak to him when I got to the end of the next chapter. I might understand more at that point.

He offered me a box of chocolate-chunk biscuits. Phil said that he was more than happy to hold the fort, if I wanted to pop out. Len suggested again that I might like to drop round to his place – a cup of tea? He couldn't offer a bath because of the water shortages, but he did have a couple of buckets. Wouldn't that be lovely? I didn't think it would be lovely. I saw Len now as he was. Cider with Len? I have a vivid imagination, but there are limits. He was a builder with ragged hands and a pot belly, plus a boring habit of talking about the benefits of combi boilers and the challenges of his teeth.

*

The vicar came to visit. I was reading *Pride and Prejudice* by then – but the vicar *did* actually come for tea. I'd heard he was concerned about the people camping on our lawn. Tents had been put up out in the street now as well. People were hanging around, sitting in circles, banging drums, chanting and praying. Bunches of flowers were propped up against the wall under the window and the curtains were still closed.

Phil insisted that I stop reading and talk to the vicar. I'd never met the man before, even though the church is on our street. I didn't want Carmen to be part of that conversation, but I could find no way to get rid of her. So I explained to the vicar that, in all honesty, the whole thing was her fault. She'd told people about our reader and suggested to them that he was a spiritual leader when, in reality, there was no reason to think that.

I agreed with the vicar that it was hard to explain why people had started to think that a man in a bedroom reading books was the path to our salvation. We both felt that it was probably because the circumstances were so difficult. People thought they were being punished and they wanted to find a way to be forgiven. In reality, they were being conned, misled, hoodwinked.

I said this in front of Carmen. I didn't care. You read *The Portrait of a Lady* and you understand how women have been trapped by men. Admittedly, it was a woman, Carmen, who had trapped me in this particular case – but it's the same point. Carmen was most annoyed and went into a rant about medieval hermits and anchorites. I think it was Dostoyevsky and his monk who started her off on that one. Now she was reading Julian of Norwich.

She started to explain to the vicar about anchorites and how they live in tiny cells with only a hole through which food is passed. They were often powerful women in the past. The vicar tried to cut her off, but still she went on about how our reader was a holy man and the people on our lawn were responding at a deep level to his goodness and his sacrifice. All of this was evidence that the Second Coming was at hand. Four horsemen had been seen at the end of our road.

'They were police horses,' I said. '*Police horses.*'

The vicar was polite to Carmen. He did not doubt her sincerity. Of course, God does work in mysterious ways. Who could say whether the Second Coming might happen in Swindon? Carmen was right that we were all searching for salvation. But there are many ways to serve God. Often what is needed is practical action. For example, he hoped that Carmen would come to Sunday service. Help was particularly needed on the church cleaning rota as everywhere was just so dusty now. He was sure that we could see his point.

I could, actually. But what was I to do? I'd told all those people to go away. Phil came in and told the vicar just how difficult it was for us. The garden was being ruined. We were not people who liked to be the centre of attention. I used the example of *The Great Gatsby*. Gatsby was famous but also private. He could manage both because he lived in a big house and probably had security gates. It was not so easy for us. I poured the vicar another cup of tea, even though it tasted of dirty river and there was no milk.

*

We were waiting for everything to get back to normal. We knew it would happen soon. We'd all been told that preparations had been made for when problems of this type started to happen more frequently, but now we were wondering whether that had ever been true. People were beginning to suspect that the government could give Dan Brown a run for his money when it came to telling improbable stories.

A group of people in the street decided to set up a committee and some work groups. This was happening up and down the country. You couldn't just leave it to the borough council. They hadn't the staff or the planning. One of the first things the committee decided was that everyone who was a visitor to the area should leave. With resources becoming so scarce, it just wasn't possible to find water for everyone.

I was appalled, but most people agreed. Even Jamila was in favour, and she worked as a volunteer at the refugee centre. Even the vicar, for God's sake. You find out you don't know people at all. The clock had definitely struck thirteen. Anyway, in reality that plan wasn't likely to come to much, because who could make it happen?

What power did the committees have? Everywhere people were talking but nothing happened.

*

The reader kept getting through the books. *Great Expectations. The Count of Monte Cristo. Tender Is the Night. One Flew Over the Cuckoo's Nest.* Susan felt that the books he was reading were more and more unpleasant. Those kinds of books gave no nourishment to the soul. He shouldn't encourage others in laziness. Jamila was also concerned. He'd been in that room for six weeks now. *One Flew Over the Cuckoo's Nest*? He was obviously ill.

Ill? She wasn't considering cause and effect. If you've got more than one hundred religious lunatics outside your window, then it can drive you fairly close to the edge. I held *Great Expectation*s up close to my face and blocked her out. But I was worried about our reader as well. I knew his secret, knew that he had to keep himself hidden. But how much longer could he do that? Look at what happened to Gatsby.

More and more people were camped out in our street. I had to hide his washing in the cupboard under the stairs so that people couldn't get their hands on it. At first, everyone at the library had been thrilled that so many people were taking out books, but then a man in Lydiard Millicent fell down the stairs while reading and broke his neck. Soon the librarians' delight turned to worry as there were hardly any books left on the shelves. Our reader and I both knew what it was like when you became the centre of too much attention. Soon I would be able to talk to him and he would understand.

*

The tarmac on the road melted and the heat hit forty-five degrees. The power went off with a dull electric sizzle, the image on the TV shrinking to a grey hole before everything went black. You couldn't even get the radio on. Phil and I went round the house pushing the switches again and again because we couldn't get used to the idea that nothing was working. The mob out on the lawn were sure that the power would never come back on. Vengeance is mine, says the Lord.

Spare me, please. I went back to the sitting room. Later I became aware that Susan had entered the room, but I just pressed *The Count of Monte Cristo* closer to my face. She was telling me that she had bad news, very bad news, that I needed to prepare myself. Probably she was worried that she wouldn't be able to finish her literature course now that the power was off. She grabbed the book and pulled it away from my face.

She told me then that Len had been killed by a falling bookcase. It was probably caused by all the cracks opening up in walls and ceilings. Someone in the street had heard a crashing sound and, when they saw what had happened, they had run to find Jamila. She had done her best to help him. Maybe he could have survived if they had been able to get him to the hospital, but Jamila had said there was no point in taking him there. People were already laid out all along the corridors and not much could be done with the power off.

I put the *Count* back in front of my face. Really, if you are called Len then you probably should be careful of standing too close to bookcases. Had he not realised this might happen? He should have read more books. How can you know about the world if you don't read?

'Don't you care?' Susan said.

'Some types of people have the means to live a culturally enriching life and others do not. Attempts to help impoverished people may make their situation worse.'

That's what I had discovered from reading Forster.

She grabbed the book from me and started shouting. 'What are you doing? You can't do nothing all day. You and all these other people just lazing around reading books – can't you see what's happening? You aren't even interested in books. You just fancy him, don't you? You don't care about poor Len. Or Phil. You never cared about either of them. Don't you think it's time to stop being so selfish?'

I grabbed the Count back and blocked her out.

'Don't you see how you've changed?' she said.

For a moment my mind did fix on those words. Had I changed? Was she right? The sour slant of her mouth drove that thought away. Frankly, if I'd been married to her, I'd have been looking to improve my French. She's as boring and self-righteous as Jane Eyre. Mr Rochester should have stuck with that mad woman in the attic, he really should.

'You need to hand the reader over,' she said. 'You know you do.'

'Just because some committee says so? They're not the government.'

'They are now.'

'I thought you were the one who wanted everyone to read?'

'I was. But haven't you noticed, haven't you seen?'

I just wanted to get back to the Count and his daring escape.

'I'll tell the committee about him,' Susan said.

'No, you won't. Now get out of here.'

*

She *would* report me. That was the problem. I would have to do what the committee said. Staying in bed all day reading had become a crime. Everyone had to join a work group. People everywhere were listening to what the committees said as there was no other government now. How could there be when we had no means of communicating with London? But I had a plan, and Dumas had helped me finalise the details. If the Count of Monte Cristo could swim out of his chateau-prison, it must be possible to get out of Hunter's Grove.

The petrol stations had shut down and no one could use a car. People had even been asked to siphon out whatever petrol they had in order to keep the ambulances running, but that had only lasted for a day or two. Phil always had a spare can of petrol on the beam in the garage – he was that kind of man. So it was all easy enough.

We'd drive to some place where the power was on and find somewhere to stay. Maybe a good B&B – or perhaps a gamekeeper's cottage. Even an attic would do. My escape plans might have been sketchy, but I knew that the nights would certainly be tender. I'd imagined them in some detail. We could not delay too long. It might be best to leave that night, after everyone was asleep. I packed my bag and made myself ready. I took plenty of books and all the notes I had made. Once we were away, I would start on the novel I wanted to write.

That night something strange happened. Or at least, it wasn't strange, but it had come to seem strange – very strange. It was rain, just rain. It didn't come with any drama; there was no warning. Just a feathery scattering of fine rain – but as it came down great shouts of relief sounded all about. Out in the garden, those who were camping raised their hands and reached for the rain, smeared it on their faces, hugged each other and wept. The Lord's Prayer was being repeated again and again.

I knew then that something had fractured, that change was coming. The moment was upon us. Phil was outside trying to protect the garden again. I checked to see that the petrol can was there. As I was lifting it down, I found a torch standing beside it. I flicked it on and then off again. Good old Phil. I found the car keys, took the torch, went up the back stairs to find our reader. The tray I'd left earlier was outside the door. The screwed-up paper napkin, the remains of sweetcorn and peas, a smear of risotto still on the side of the plate.

I stood staring at that tray for a long moment, then moved towards the door. I was doing this for his own good. I needed to save him. The pressure he'd been placed under was too much. I knocked quietly on the door and waited. From outside, I heard more shouting and laughter, the words of a hymn swelling and falling, but there was no sound from within the room. I knocked again and waited. I pressed my ear up against the door but I couldn't hear a sound. Finally, I pushed the handle down and eased the door open just an inch. I was hoping that would alert him to my presence, but he didn't come to the door.

'Excuse me, excuse me. Are you there?'

I might have felt annoyed at his refusal to respond, but I knew he must be reading. He was probably into the last chapter of *Jane Eyre*. He was blind, he was damaged, but soon he would feel me close and realise that the woman he had always wanted was right there beside him. I pushed the door a little further and called again. It was no good. I'd have to go in and stand right in front of him. I swung the door wide. The room was dark, the window was open. He'd sometimes opened it a crack before, but now it was hanging wide open. Maybe he also wanted to feel the rain.

I stepped forward towards the bed and called out to him again. 'Excuse me, excuse me.' I started to explain that we needed to leave, to let him know my plan. He said nothing. I thought about putting my hand out to touch him. I wanted to go and draw back the curtain, but I didn't want the people on the lawn to see. Instead I switched on the torch. Its light flickered madly across the wall and the ceiling. From outside I heard a great cheer rise up from the garden. The circular light from the torch came to rest on the bed.

Reader, he had gone. I spun the torch around. I walked to the bathroom, but he wasn't there. I pulled open the wardrobe door, looked behind the armchair, got down on my hands and knees and looked under the bed. Nothing. No one at all. The bed a little crumpled, the window open, the room musty and close. Some dirty socks left on the chair. Other than that – nothing.

It was impossible. Impossible. They say that in moments of crisis people are often extremely calm. I turned into Phil – I became a detective. I went to the open window and looked out. I could see blurry footmarks on the roof of the garden room. His feet were slightly wet from the rain and so the marks stood out from the patterns of individual drops. There was no doubt about it.

While everyone had been busy collecting rainwater with buckets and Tupperware, he had simply climbed down onto the roof below. Lucky, really, that he hadn't fallen through, given the state of that roof. I turned and walked downstairs, shivering violently, as though a fever had seized me. Outside there was still that same business everywhere – tubs and saucers and buckets and dustbins. All being lined up. Crowds of people were looking up at the window. The light, the light. They'd seen the light.

Since everyone was still focused on the window, they didn't see me. I hurried to the gate that leads into the alleyway. The air was white and misty because of the rain. I looked down at the path and there, in the dust, were footmarks. I hurried up to the next street and my eyes searched all around. Crowds of people were out, wild-eyed and crackling with laughter, some wearing pyjamas, some in their underwear, all of them trying to catch the water. Footprints were leading away down the road and I decided that they must be his. I don't know now if they really were. But I knew then that everything was shattered and that I would never see him again. The common sense of the morning would bring no relief.

*

That should have been the end of it. He was a cheap con man who owed me £600. He'd taken several library books with him and they'd been signed out on my card. The pair of socks he'd left behind smelled of sweaty feet. There was no mystery, no romance, no salvation. He was an ordinary man reading books. We had been duped, tricked, in cold blood.

But the problem with stories is that, once they've started, they can be hard to stop. They gather speed like a boulder hurtling downhill. People were not in the mood for facts. It was a time of madness and hysteria. Sparks of rumour, gossip and false information were blown in on that hot wind from the Sahara, setting the town alight. Once again, it was Carmen who caused all the problems.

This was the empty tomb and the Messiah had gone. He'd been sent to show us the way, to lead us to the light, to save us from our harsh and cruel world. He'd been called back to his heavenly home where he would pray for us sinners left behind on earth. She'd known him, she'd served him, she'd washed his feet. She would take his place and become his representative on earth. She went into the garden room and locked the door, pulled down all the blinds, barricaded herself in with my cane sofa. Only one window was left partially open so that food could be passed to her. She would pray for us and intercede on our behalf. Our own local anchorite. All could be saved if they only worshipped her.

Soon crowds of people were coming to lay flowers outside the garden room. Phil's roses were trampled on. Carmen had been sent to prepare us all for the Second Coming. Or the Age of Aquarius or the journey to the lost city of Atlantis. She was a new John the Baptist because, of course, in our feminist age, it was quite logical that old-time saints should reappear as women. Haven't you heard of her? The female Saint Swindon, who saves us all from the apocalypse? Don't you know your Bible? You should read it. You'll find it all in there.

*

I had been felled with an axe. My body was broken into bits so that I could hardly stand. Nothing is so painful to the human mind as a great and sudden change. But I was not going to drink poison or throw myself under a train. Particularly as the trains were not running. Finishing yourself off is quite difficult when you come to consider the practicalities. In real life, people just have to haul themselves out of bed in the morning, get the washing machine on, cook the meals. Although since there was no electricity and no gas, I couldn't do any of that. I had never thought I'd regret the death of housework.

Jamila was the one who saved me. For days I had sat on my chair in the sitting room, unable to move. Jamila came to sit opposite me and held my hand. 'We need you, Janey. We need everyone. I'm a nurse – I can teach you what I know.'

'A nurse? What? Like Lara in *Doctor Zhivago*?'

'No, Janey. Like in real life. You know, actual life.'

It occurred to me then that I'd never actually liked Jamila, but she wouldn't let the matter rest, so finally I did as she said. So there I was, signed up by the work groups, although I'd spent a lifetime avoiding do-gooders. At least that left me with no time to think. Thinking was not a good idea.

I could let all of it go. I had to, there was no choice – but Phil could not. I don't think it was the roses that broke him. In reality, he'd known for a while that the garden was doomed. What made him angry was that no one had listened to him. He'd known all along that the man was a criminal and his suspicions had been proven right. He had all the evidence assembled. So he went to the police station and told them all that had happened.

He wanted me to go with him but I couldn't face it, so Jamila went instead. Of course, the police couldn't search any of their databases as the computers were all down. Anyway, they were quick to point out that the name Jack MacKafka was clearly invented. 'Really, sir? It didn't occur to you that no one actually has a name like that?'

No, it had not occurred to Phil or anyone else. They asked Phil for an address and, of course, he didn't have one. A photograph? No, unfortunately not. Phil did have fingerprints and he knew all about the forensic evidence that would be needed. His knowledge of DNA and ballistics was impressive. He had all his books there with him, and all the relevant pages were marked with Post-it notes. He started to take the police through it all in some detail, failing to notice that they were laughing at him.

'Never a good idea to read too many crime books,' they said.

Anyway, £600 wasn't much money and we could pursue our reader through the small claims courts. It might be best to tighten up our check-in procedures, to be sure to ask for identification in future. Phil fought back, tried to make them take action.

'Now really, sir. I think you'd do best to leave this alone. After all, you and your wife were allowing a visitor to stay in your house long after the committees had decided that all visitors must leave. I'm sure you don't want me to question your loyalty.'

The police officer also hoped that he did not need to remind Phil that the consequences could be dire for those who put their own interests above those of the country in this moment of crisis. Phil was made to look a fool. Of course, he is a fool – I've always known that – but still, I didn't want it shoved in my face.

*

Only Carmen seemed unable to grasp what had happened. The committees told her and the mob in the street that they needed to sign up for work. But Carmen couldn't have cared less about the committees because her eyes were fixed on some larger salvation. Ragged groups of people were still walking in across the fields, arriving dusty and tearful, desperate for some comfort. Hunter's Grove was entirely surrounded – the street was choked with people, there was wailing and hugging.

It was Susan who brought it all to an end – with the help of the vicar. She went to the committees and told them that Saint Swindon was all just a con. The whole scam had been started by a man staying in bed and reading books. Carmen had never even seen him. The committees understood, but still they hesitated to take action. In such difficult times, people surely needed to believe in something?

The vicar added his voice. Belief was important, but so was practical action. God wasn't going to help anyone who didn't help themselves. It wasn't just the graveyard and the church flowers now. The need was vast and urgent. God was calling each and every one of us to do vital work to keep us all alive. Our Lord needed buckets of water, not chanting.

The committees came and cleared everyone out of our garden, put them all to work. Most went willingly, but some were stubborn. In the end, they had to get sticks and drive them off. Still there was Carmen herself, the holy Saint Swindon boarded up in our garden room. The vicar went in there and had a long conversation with her. They agreed that she would leave the town. She still had a few faithful followers and they stayed with her as she emerged.

She kissed the ground and then walked away. People said later that she was carrying a staff. Actually it was our garden rake. Others were carrying wooden crosses in front of them. Carmen said to me that a prophet is never received in her own town. She would pray for me. I ignored her. What good would prayers do? How much more evidence did any of us need that there is no God? The Holocaust passed Him by, so what hope for Swindon? Yet still I stood and watched until they all reached the end of the road and turned out of sight.

*

Winter came and never went. Five long years have passed and occasionally a feeble sun shines, but summer never comes. We live now in the gaps between stories. Not exactly *Darkness at Noon*, but certainly clouds of ash as thick as curtains. For six months of each year we live in Arctic conditions. Everyone has moved out of their houses and we live huddled together in the church. A fire burns night and day and is used for cooking as well as warmth. We work all day carrying water. Every inch of the earth is planted with vegetables – even the tarmac where the roads once were has been dug up. This is a nightmare from which we will not wake.

The books are long gone. They were needed for fuel. Not one voice was raised in protest. Every single book was brought to the church and piled up there. Susan helped to organise that. Initially the pages were stripped out one by one and thrown on the fire, the flames licking across each line of text. But then someone pointed out that you could get more heat if you burned them whole, so that's what we did. The last one to go was *The Road* by Cormac McCarthy. Someone did argue that we should keep that book, but they got no support. You lose interest in dystopia when it's on your doorstep.

So much that happened was the fault of the books. Reading? Empathy? Perhaps there are some points of view we should not try to understand. You read books and you copy behaviour that shouldn't be copied. You speak in words that are not your own. You think you are powerful, you become a Messiah in your own mind. Books make us think that we can change, but we can't. We just become more of what we always were. We tell the same stories over and over again. We do not learn lessons. The world is not a puzzle that we can solve.

Occasionally ragged strangers arrive at the church, wildfires burning in their eyes, and through them we hear news of Carmen and the many miracles she has worked. Apparently, she put her staff – or garden rake – into the ground in Wimbledon and water spouted out of the earth. Everyone smirked when they heard that. We are no longer people who believe in fanciful ideas. The age of miracles has long passed.

We live in a time of frenetic stagnation. Sometimes there is a feeling of surging hope, of euphoria. People talk in tones of whispered wonder about how we used to live. Shopping centres and cars, safe, warm lives. But were we not all anaesthetised? Were we not all half dead? Perhaps now we have been set free into something wild and fierce. We are becoming our animal selves, recovering the lost wildness within.

On some days you can believe this. But mostly it is work and dirt and hunger and fear. *Good Morning, Midnight*. Perhaps the worst part is the silence all around. We have no idea if the rest of the country, or the rest of the world, still exists. News sometimes comes to us from neighbouring communities, but we know nothing of what might be happening twenty miles away. The nights are the worst. You forget what you want to remember and remember what you want to forget. In the church you can hear people all around you weeping in the fire-lit shadows. *Heart of Darkness*? We're living it now.

Jamila often moves around among those crying people, offering comfort or wise advice. She is needed, loved. I say that in all sincerity. The days when we used to mock kindness are finished. Phil has also become a vital member of our community. A different kind of saint. He organises the planting, harvesting and distribution of the few crops we grow. We need the kind of man who keeps a spare can of petrol on the beam in the garage, who can grow a potato as well as a rose. We value the labour of fools now.

*

The year is 2035. One morning, the committee tells us that we need more carpet. The temperature is sinking ever lower. The church must be packed with more insulation if we are to survive. As this is discussed, it occurs to me that the carpets may not have been taken out of the front upstairs rooms at Hunter's Grove. I volunteer to go and take a look, to see what I can find. In truth, I offer partly because I have a yearning now to go back to the house. I haven't been there for many months.

As I walk through the grey light, I keep watch all around me. I have a large, sharp knife at the ready because of the wolves, and I am wrapped in several blankets. The house is dusty; the windows hang open, the front door broken down. Nearly everything has been stripped from the rooms. Some things were carried to the church, but much was taken by the marauders who looted this area in those first days after the Great Heat, when terror made us cruel. Oddly, the hall mirror is still hanging and as I pass it I catch sight of myself. I've turned into the mad woman in the attic. I've got my waist back.

I move first towards the front stairs, but then turn and hesitate at the bottom of the back stairs. Surely the carpet was taken from that room. I shouldn't go up those stairs – but I do. Hesitating on the landing, I stop and listen, but there's nothing to be heard. No one has been in that room since the day he departed. The papers

I left there, my notes, are still lying on the desk, covered with dust. I remember how much I liked writing those notes, how I thought I'd write a book. It was evening when the stranger arrived in the town.

Kafka. MacKafka. Truth be told, I hadn't understood *The Castle* at all. Where was the story? Now I understand it rather too well. We are going round and round. It will not end. There is no sense to it. It's not just that you don't know other people, you don't know yourself either. But I mustn't think about that. Part of the bedroom wall has collapsed, leaving a gaping hole up to the ceiling. The floral wallpaper is speckled with mould. The bed and the wardrobe have gone, but a chair and the carpet remain. I ease up carpet tacks with the side of the knife.

As I pull the carpet back, I see that one of the floorboards underneath is loose. I edge my fingers down into a crack and raise the board. Something is hidden down below. Two books, lying face down far below the boards. He must have put them there. I draw back from them. Ownership of books is an offence. How can you own books when people are dying from the cold? I'll hand them in as soon as I get back to the church.

I reach down to take them out. Please, not a nineteenth-century novel. I've done realism now, seen it from every angle, and it's got nothing to recommend it. I turn over the first book. Strangely, it's a children's book which I remember from when I was young. They made a film out of it, back in that other world.

Stick to the facts, hold on to the here and now. We were so busy reading between the lines that we forgot to read the lines themselves. We were a generation overloaded with knowledge, dying of ignorance. I mustn't, I mustn't. But Jack MacKafka is here again now, standing close. I pull my blankets around me, sit down, start to read. The words are like nectar, like honey. They tempt, capture, beguile, excite. Like fire, like water, like fresh air. They are our element.

Carmen. She was a fraud and a fantasist. I haven't changed my mind about that. All that ridiculous stuff she believed. What an idiot she was. But was I any better? Carmen understood, at least, that you can't live on facts alone. Particularly when the facts turn out to be less factual than they first appeared. You may not need the word of God, but you do need something beyond the everyday. I think now of what she said – how can you build the future if you do not dream?

Will we always live now in cold, hunger and loss? Or can we find a way to start again? Dreams as salvation, dreams as damnation. Any plans for the day? I think I'll just sit in this chair and read. The cold and the horror drop away and the words take me in their arms and hold me tight. We'd all like to walk through the back of a wardrobe and into a forest where a street lamp burns bright.

List of Books

Alexander Dumas, *The Count of Monte Cristo*
Arthur Koestler, *Darkness at Noon*
Boris Pasternak, *Doctor Zhivago*
Charles Dickens, *Great Expectations*
Charlotte Brontë, *Jane Eyre*
Cormac McCarthy, *The Road*
D. H. Lawrence, *Lady Chatterley's Lover*
Donna Tartt, *The Secret History*
E. M. Forster, *Howards End*
F. Scott Fitzgerald, *The Great Gatsby*
F. Scott Fitzgerald, *Tender Is the Night*
F. Scott Fitzgerald, *The Crack-up*
Franz Kafka, *The Castle*
Fyodor Dostoyevsky, *Crime and Punishment*
Fyodor Dostoyevsky, *The Brothers Karamazov*
George Orwell, *Animal Farm*
George Orwell, *1984*
Gustave Flaubert, *Madame Bovary*
Henry James, *The Portrait of a Lady*
Jane Austen, *Pride and Prejudice*

Jean Rhys, *Good Morning, Midnight*
Joseph Conrad, *Heart of Darkness*
Ken Kesey, *One Flew Over the Cuckoo's Nest*
Laurie Lee, *Cider with Rosie*
Sylvia Plath, *The Bell Jar*
Thomas Hardy, *Far from the Madding Crowd*
Thomas Hardy, *Tess of the d'Urbervilles*
William Makepeace Thackeray, *Vanity Fair*
W. Somerset Maugham, *Liza of Lambeth*

Afterword

Dear reader,

Thank you for reading A Saint in Swindon and thank you also to the Swindon Artswords reading group for helping me create this story. When Matt Holland first suggested that I might write a story for the group, I was more than a little nervous. I did not see myself as the obvious person for the job. What if the group simply did not like my approach?

My first meeting with them did little to calm my nerves. They welcomed me warmly and our discussions were lively and interesting, but their reading tastes were dangerously varied. Ann Patchett, O. Henry, Katherine Mansfield, Thomas Hardy, Saki, Jorge Luis Borges. How could I appeal to so many different audiences?

I was also uncertain about how our planned 'editorial meeting' would work. Although the world of the internet has brought many gifts, it has also perhaps weakened our reading culture. Readers' online comments can too often be limited to 'like' or 'dislike'. The book is sometimes treated merely as a consumer product. Certain readers ask only: did it give me what I want or not?

I should not have worried. Our 'editorial meeting' was respectful, challenging, thoughtful and honest. We were all there together, shut up in a room (or former calf shed). No escape. We had no choice but to get down to the nuts and bolts of the job. Is this character credible? Why does this happen? Can the story be changed in this way or that?

I explained to the group that, as a writer, I feel that I own the words but that the reader owns the white spaces around the words. I always want to be as generous as I can to the reader. That means leaving as much white space as possible and working on the assumption that the reader is highly intelligent. The group agreed that what was left out would be as important as what stayed in.

So busy were we – discussing, explaining and debating – that we failed to notice that some strange alchemy had entered the process. The members of the group were no longer consumers but creators. They had an emotional investment in the story. As for me, I was reminded that the so-called average reader is incredibly diverse, unpredictable and surprising. They are also much braver and more adventurous than we generally think.

We were also all reminded that the simple act of reading is a truly amazing process. It is both intensely solitary and amazingly sociable. The reader not only encounters the writer, he or she also meets all the characters who inhabit the story. Beyond that, the reader also engages with all the other people who have read the story – or who might read it in the future. The writing is remade again and again as it is considered.

I am thrilled that this story, which we created together, will now have a wider audience. And no, I'm not going to tell you what you should think about it. The white space is yours and I know you will fill it with your own questions, thoughts and images. Welcome to the conversation. Make this story your own. Enjoy the magic – and the danger – of the written word.

Alice Jolly

Author Bio

Alice Jolly's most recent novel *Mary Ann Sate, Imbecile* was published in 2018 by Unbound. It was runner-up for the Rathbones Folio Prize, was on the longlist for the Ondaatje Prize and was also selected as a Walter Scott Prize recommended novel. Alice has also won the PEN Ackerley Prize for her memoir and the V. S. Pritchett Memorial Prize for one of her short stories. She teaches creative writing at Oxford University.

Book club and writers' circle notes for
A Saint in Swindon can be found at
www.fairlightbooks.com

Share your thoughts about the
book with **#SaintInSwindon**

SOPHIE VAN LLEWYN

Bottled Goods

*Longlisted for The Women's Prize for Fiction 2019,
People's Book Prize for Fiction 2018 and The Republic
of Consciousness Prize 2019*

When Alina's brother-in-law defects to the West,
she and her husband become persons of interest to
the secret services and both of their careers come
grinding to a halt.

As the strain takes its toll on their marriage,
Alina turns to her aunt for help – the wife of a
communist leader and a secret practitioner of the
old folk ways.

Set in 1970s communist Romania, this novella-
in-flash draws upon magic realism to weave a
captivating tale of everyday troubles.

*'It is a story to savour, to smile at, to rage against
and to weep over.'*
—Zoe Gilbert, author of FOLK

*'Sophie van Llewyn's stunning debut novella
shows us there is no dystopian fiction as frighten-
ing as that which draws on history.'* —Christina
Dalcher, author of VOX

NIAL GIACOMELLI

The Therapist

*'I am levitating above the curvature of the earth.
Weightless, unencumbered. Flung like a comet out of
the atmosphere to drift eternally along the firmament.'*

In this bittersweet and hauntingly surreal tale, a
couple finds the distance between them mirrored
in a strange epidemic sweeping the globe. Little by
little, each victim becomes transparent, their heart
beating behind a visible rib cage, an intricate
network of nerves left hanging in mid-air. Finally,
the victims disappear entirely, never to be
seen again.

'I dreamt we were at sea,' she says.

*'If the population of the world had vanished
while I was reading Nial Giacomelli's beautifully
observed novella, I'm not sure I would have
noticed. It's that good.'* —Christopher Stanley,
author of *The Forest is Hungry.*'

ANTHONY FERNER

Inside the Bone Box

'On a good day at work, the tips of his fingers seemed to tingle with focused energy. They sensed the space, rose, turned through angles, intuited the tissue, felt the consistency of flesh, used just the right degree of delicacy or brutality.'

Nicholas Anderton is a highly respected neurosurgeon at the top of his field. But behind the successful façade all is not well. Tormented by a toxic marriage and haunted by past mistakes, Anderton has been eating to forget. His wife, meanwhile, has turned to drink.

There are sniggers behind closed doors – how can a surgeon be fat? When mistakes are made and his old adversary steps in to take advantage, Anderton knows things are coming to a head…

'A little book that packs a punch far greater than its size.' —The Idle Woman, blogger